KIDS' SPORTS STORIES

TENNIS TEAM TENSION

by Elliott Smith

illustrated by Amanda Erb

PICTURE WINDOW BOOKS
a capstone imprint

Published by Picture Window Books, an imprint of Capstone
1710 Roe Crest Drive, North Mankato, Minnesota 56003
capstonepub.com

Library of Congress Cataloging-in-Publication Data
Names: Smith, Elliott, 1976- author.
Title: Tennis team tension / Elliott Smith.
Other titles: Kids' sports stories.
Description: North Mankato, Minnesota : Picture Window Books,
an imprint of Capstone, [2022] | Series: Kids' sports stories | Audience:
Ages 5-7. |
Audience: Grades K-1. | Summary: Moses prefers video games to sports,
but his parents have signed him up for the tennis team anyway; his
strategy is to take it easy and hope he gets tossed from the team--his
attitude angers the other children and after one of the boys, Xavier,
gives him a lesson in teamwork, Moses finally starts to take tennis and
the team seriously. Includes suggestions for activities and discussion.
Identifiers: LCCN 2021023358 (print) | LCCN 2021023359 (ebook) | ISBN
9781663959379 (hardcover) | ISBN 9781666331899 (paperback) | ISBN
9781666331905 (pdf)
Subjects: LCSH: Tennis stories. | African American boys--Juvenile fiction.
| Teamwork (Sports)--Juvenile fiction. | Attitude (Psychology)--Juvenile
fiction. | CYAC: Tennis--Fiction. | Teamwork (Sports)--Fiction. |
African Americans--Fiction. | LCGFT: Sports fiction. | Picture books.
Classification: LCC PZ7.1.S626 Te 2022 (print) | LCC PZ7.1.S626 (ebook)
|DDC 813.6 [E]--dc23
LC record available at https://lccn.loc.gov/2021023358
LC ebook record available at https://lccn.loc.gov/2021023359

Editorial Credits
Editor: Carrie Sheely; Designer: Bobbie Nuytten; Media Researcher:
Morgan Walters; Production Specialist: Laura Manthe

Printed in the United States   5849

TABLE OF CONTENTS

Glossary

 **backhand**—hitting the ball when the back of your hand is facing the same direction as the swing

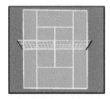 **court**—a rectangular surface where tennis is played

 **forehand**—hitting the ball when the palm of your hand is facing the same direction as the swing

 **match**—a tennis contest; a match is won when a player or team has won the majority of the sets

 **racket**—an object with netting and a handle used to hit tennis balls

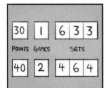 **set**—a group of games; a player must win at least six games to win a set

Chapter 1
UNPLUGGED

Moses leaned in closer to the TV. *BOINK! SKREE!* He was playing his favorite video game. He didn't even notice his parents come into the room.

"Hi, Moses," his dad said. "It's time for tennis practice. Grab your **racket**!"

Moses sighed. "Okay, Dad," Moses said. He didn't want to play tennis. But his parents thought it would be good for him to get outside. So they signed him up.

Moses was in a bad mood when his parents dropped him off for practice.

"Have fun!" his mom said. Moses scowled and dragged his feet toward the **courts**.

"Welcome to the Aces team!" said a tall man with a booming voice. "My name is Coach Howard. I hope you're looking forward to learning about tennis. We'll practice for a few weeks and then play some games."

Coach Howard started talking about **forehands** and **backhands**. But Moses wasn't paying attention. He didn't care about tennis. He just wanted to play video games.

Moses didn't try hard at practices. *I'll just show up and take it easy,* he thought. *Then maybe I can quit.*

At one practice, he saw the ball coming but just walked to it.

TWEEEET! Coach's whistle rang out. He gathered the team. "Some teammates haven't been trying very hard. So everyone else will run to make up for it."

The team moaned. They had to run laps
around the court. Moses felt bad. He looked
at his angry teammates. He knew this was
his fault.

Chapter 2

AT FAULT

Later, Moses sat on his bed playing with his racket. Mom walked in. "How was practice today?" she asked.

"I think the team is mad at me," Moses said. "I wasn't trying hard."

"You should always do your best," Mom said. "Think of it like a real-life video game."

Moses thought about what his mom said. He liked being outside. And he liked trying to win at video games. Maybe he could win at tennis too. Moses decided to try harder.

At the next practice, Moses zoomed around the court. He made good forehand shots. *WHAP!*

But he had a hard time with his backhands. He swung wildly and missed every shot.

He decided to ask some of his teammates
for help. But everyone was still mad about
the last practice.

"Why should I help you?" asked Xavier,
the star player. "You got us all in trouble."

Coach brought the team together. "We have our first tournament next Saturday," he said. "We're playing against the Slammers. We'll have singles and doubles **matches**." He started naming which teammates would play together on the doubles teams.

Shayna + Nomi
Jessica + Raquel
Xavier + Moses
Adam + Kai

". . . And our last doubles team will be Xavier and Moses," Coach said.

Moses was shocked. He looked over at Xavier. Xavier glared back. Moses gulped.

Chapter 3

WINNING TEAMWORK

Moses arrived early for the next practice. He was surprised to see Xavier already there.

"Hey, Xavier," Moses said. "I'm really sorry you all had to run because of the way I acted. I didn't want to play at first. But I do now! I promise to try my best. I'm glad you're my teammate for the tournament."

Xavier smiled. "That's okay." Xavier pointed at Moses' T-shirt. "Do you like Mega Quest? Maybe we could play together?"

"Yes! I love video games!" Moses said.
"I wish I was as good at tennis as I am at
video games. I'm still worried about my
backhand. Could you help me?"

"Sure!" Xavier said. Xavier showed Moses how to grip the racket for backhand shots. The next week, they practiced at the courts after school. Soon, Moses felt better about his backhand. When they were done practicing each day, they had fun playing video games together.

The day of the tournament arrived.

"Okay, team, let's go!" Coach said. "Xavier and Moses, you're up first."

As the match began, Xavier and Moses played well together. *WHACK!* Moses swung hard with his forehand. Xavier covered for Moses on tough balls.

Then the ball headed straight for Moses'
backhand. He tried his new swing and . . .
WHIFF! He missed the ball. The Slammers
won the first **set**. Moses dropped his head.

"That's okay," Xavier said. "We'll get
them on the next one."

Soon it was time for the final set.

Whoever won this set would win the match.

As the last game ended, Xavier ran up
to hit the ball. But he slipped! Moses would
have to hit the ball backhand. He gripped
his racket, swung, and . . . hit a perfect
shot! The Aces won!

The team ran over to celebrate. "Great job, Moses!" Xavier said.

"You too! We make a great team!" Moses said.

TENNIS DRILL FUN

Are you ready to try some fun tennis drills? You can do the frying pan and double dribble by yourself or with a friend.

What You Need:
- tennis racket
- tennis ball
- timer or stopwatch

What You Do:
- For the frying pan, hold the tennis racket in your hand and place a ball on top of it. Start moving the racket up and down until the ball bounces. Try to keep it bouncing for as long as possible.
- With double dribble, drop the ball and start bouncing it with your racket. Try to dribble for as long as possible. For an extra challenge, start moving and dribbling.
- If you're playing with a friend, see who can bounce the ball the longest for each drill.

Take another look at this illustration. How do you think Moses felt when he learned he was going to be on a team with Xavier? How do you think Xavier felt? Have you had a similar experience?

Think about what you can do if you are nervous about working with someone. Make a list of things you can do to help the experience go well.

ABOUT THE AUTHOR

Elliott Smith is a former sports reporter who covered athletes in all sports from high school to the pros. He is one of the authors of the Natural Thrills series about extreme outdoor sports. In his spare time, he likes playing sports with his two children, going to the movies, and adding to his collection of Pittsburgh Steelers memorabilia.

ABOUT THE ILLUSTRATOR

Amanda Erb is an illustrator from Maryland currently living in the Boston, Massachusetts, area. She earned a BFA in illustration from Ringling College of Art and Design. In her free time, she enjoys playing soccer, learning Spanish, and discovering new stories to read.